LIKE LAVA IN MY VEINS

DERRICK BARNES

ART BY
SHAWN MARTINBROUGH

COLORS BY
ADRIANO LUCAS

Nancy Paulsen Books

NANCY PAULSEN BOOKS
An imprint of Penguin Random House LLC, New York

First published in the United States of America by Nancy Paulsen Books,
an imprint of Penguin Random House LLC, 2023

Text copyright © 2023 by Derrick Barnes
Illustrations copyright © 2023 by Shawn Martinbrough

Visit us online at penguinrandomhouse.com.

Library of Congress Cataloging-in-Publication Data
Names: Barnes, Derrick, author. | Martinbrough, Shawn, illustrator.
Title: Like lava in my veins / Derrick Barnes ; illustrated by Shawn Martinbrough.
Description: New York : Nancy Paulsen Books, 2023.
Summary: "Bobby Beacon has trouble controlling his hot
temper at his superhero school"—Provided by publisher.
Identifiers: LCCN 2022031997 | ISBN 9780525518747 (hardcover)
ISBN 9780525518761 (ebook) | ISBN 9780525518754 (ebook)
Subjects: CYAC: Temper–Fiction. | Superheroes–Fiction.
Schools–Fiction. | LCGFT: Superhero fiction.
Picture books. Classification: LCC PZ7.B26154 Li 2023 | DDC [E]–dc23
LC record available at https://lccn.loc.gov/2022031997

Manufactured in China
ISBN 9780525518747
1 3 5 7 9 10 8 6 4 2
TOPL

Edited by Nancy Paulsen
Art direction by Marikka Tamura
Design by Dave Kopka
Text set in CCMeanwhile and CCVictorySpeechLow
All of the artwork for *Like Lava in My Veins* was drawn by hand, using a
combination of ink, crow quill, pen, and brush. The colors were painted digitally.

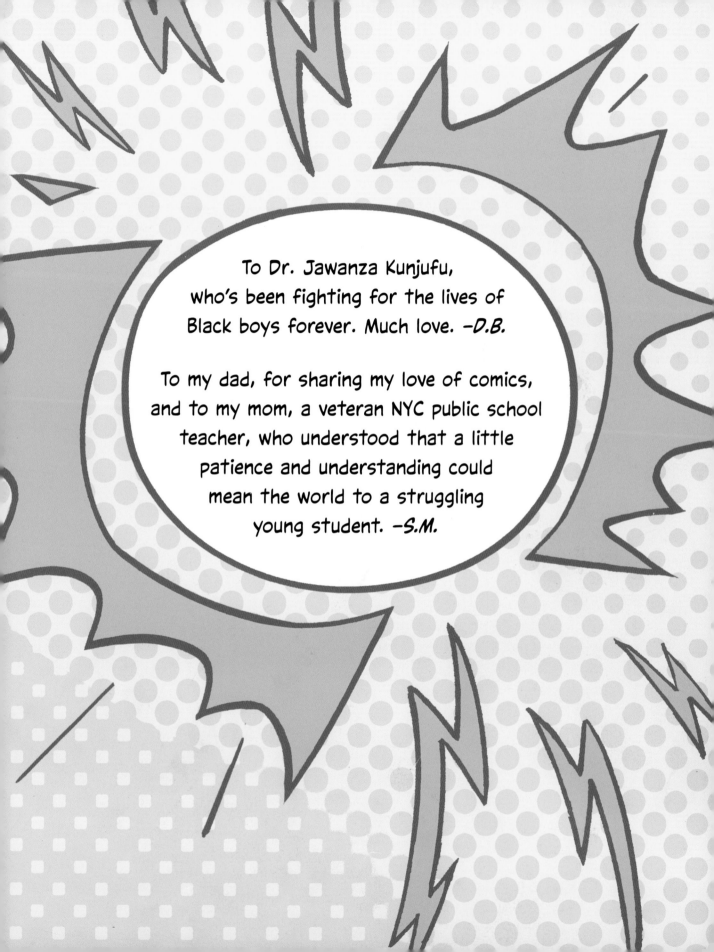

To Dr. Jawanza Kunjufu,
who's been fighting for the lives of
Black boys forever. Much love. *–D.B.*

To my dad, for sharing my love of comics,
and to my mom, a veteran NYC public school
teacher, who understood that a little
patience and understanding could
mean the world to a struggling
young student. *–S.M.*

LIKE WHEN I ALMOST MISSED THE BUS ON MY VERY FIRST DAY.

YO... HOLD UP!!

THE DRIVER SHUT THE DANG DOOR IN MY FACE—AND *LAUGHED!*

WE ARRIVED AT THE ACADEMY ON TIME. I'D NEVER SEEN ANYTHING LIKE IT.

THERE WERE GIGANTIC STATUES AND KIDS FLYING AROUND WITH EVERY SUPERPOWER IMAGINABLE.

MY FIRST WEEK AT THE SCHOOL, A GIRL NAMED *PAUSE* GOT EXPELLED FOR TURNING A TEACHER INTO A STATUE. SHE DIDN'T WANT RECESS TO END. NONE OF US DID.

ALL SHE DID WAS SING.

JUST FLOATED A COUPLE OF SWEET NOTES IN THE AIR THAT LANDED SOFTLY IN THE EAR OF A FIFTH-GRADE TEACHER NAMED MR. REMINGTON—HE WAS FROZEN SOLID.

PAUSE'S PARENTS ENDED UP IN PRINCIPAL WESTVIEW'S OFFICE.

WE TRIED SO HARD TO GET HER POWERS UNDER CONTROL. BUT PAUSE IS JUST ONE OF THOSE KIDS...

SHE'S *IMPOSSIBLE* TO REACH.

IT WAS JUST HER FIRST WEEK, SO I DON'T THINK THEY TRIED HARD ENOUGH.

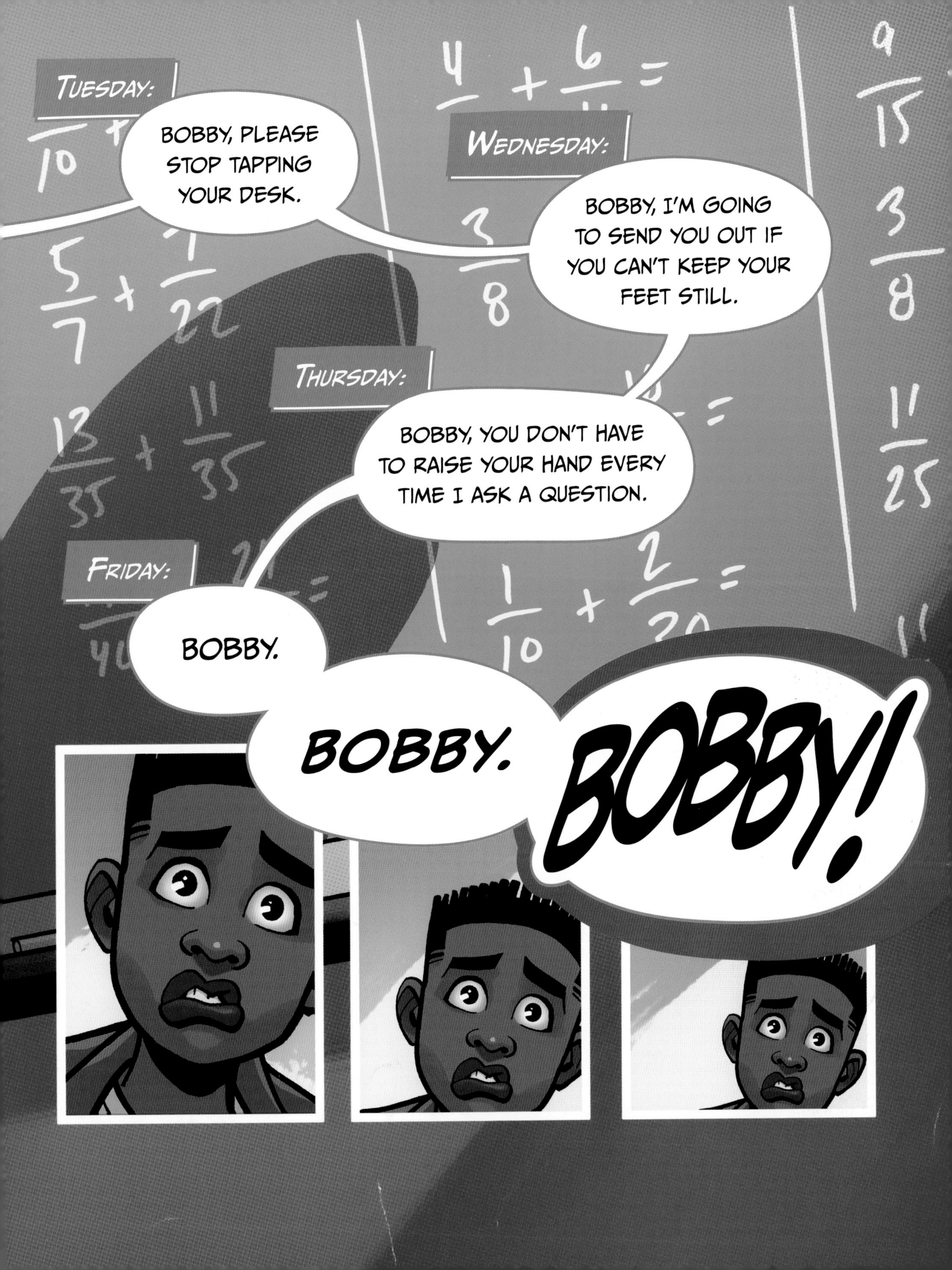
TUESDAY:
BOBBY, PLEASE STOP TAPPING YOUR DESK.
WEDNESDAY:
BOBBY, I'M GOING TO SEND YOU OUT IF YOU CAN'T KEEP YOUR FEET STILL.
THURSDAY:
BOBBY, YOU DON'T HAVE TO RAISE YOUR HAND EVERY TIME I ASK A QUESTION.
FRIDAY:
BOBBY.
BOBBY.
BOBBY!

I ENDED UP IN PRINCIPAL WESTVIEW'S OFFICE.

BOBBY, I KNOW GETTING USED TO A NEW SCHOOL IS TOUGH, BUT YOU CAN'T DESTROY SCHOOL PROPERTY.

IF YOU CAN'T LEARN TO CONTROL YOURSELF, YOU COULD END UP WHERE PAUSE IS— *THE INSTITUTE FOR SUPERVILLAINS.*

APPARENTLY, THEY'RE EAGER FOR NEW TALENT...

SHE HAD A CLUSTER OF FRECKLES AROUND HER NOSE, JUST LIKE MY MOM. SHE EVEN WORE HER HAIR UP IN A WRAP, LIKE MY MOM.

AND JUST LIKE ME, SHE LOVED LANGSTON HUGHES.

"Look at my face – dark as the night – Yet shining like the sun with love's true light." – LH

WHEN I GOT FRUSTRATED WITH A MATH PROBLEM AND MY TEMPERATURE BEGAN TO RISE, MISS BROOKLYN CALMED ME DOWN WITH HER SOOTHING VOICE.

CLOSE YOUR EYES, BOBBY, AND TAKE FIVE DEEP BREATHS.

INHALE AND EXHALE SLOWLY. NOW OPEN YOUR EYES AND SAY TO YOURSELF, *PEACE, BE STILL...*

I DID WHAT SHE SAID, AND IT WORKED! THE BRIGHT ORANGE LAVA THAT COULD USUALLY BE SEEN PUMPING THROUGH MY VEINS CALMED ALL THE WAY DOWN.

MISS BROOKLYN MADE US A SPACE WITH BOOKS, MAGAZINES, A LITTLE FOUNTAIN, AND BEANBAG CHAIRS THAT SHE CALLED "THE CHILL ZONE."

SINCERE IS A FUNNY DUDE. HE'LL ASK YOU A QUESTION LIKE:

YOU GOT ANY MORE JELLY BEANS?

UMM...NO. ALL GONE, MAN.

HERE'S THE THING—IF YOU HAVE SOME, YOU CAN'T SAY THAT YOU DON'T. ALL HE HAS TO DO IS TOUCH YOU, AND THE TRUTH JUST COMES POURING OUT OF YOUR MOUTH LIKE NIAGARA FALLS.

REALLY? NONE?

...I JUST BOUGHT A WHOLE BAG. A BIG ONE, TOO. WANT SOME?

THAT'S HIS POWER. YOU CAN'T FRONT ON SINCERE. HE MAKES YOU TELL THE WHOLE TRUTH. PERIOD.

HEY, YOU WON'T EVER HAVE TO WORRY ABOUT ME TELLING YOU THE TRUTH. THAT'S WHAT FRIENDS DO.

YOU KNOW, I'VE BEEN HERE FOR TWO YEARS, AND I'VE NEVER REALLY HAD A REAL FRIEND. LIKE...EVER.

WELL, BROTHER, YOU'VE GOT ONE NOW. BELIEVE THAT.

I STARTED TO TAKE PRIDE IN MY SCHOOL, AND I EVEN STARTED WEARING THE ACADEMY GEAR. BUT ONE DAY, THE INSTITUTE MESSED AROUND AND CAME LOOKING FOR ME!

WE WERE IN THE AUDITORIUM FOR AN AWARDS ASSEMBLY.

STUDENTS, TODAY WE RECOGNIZE THOSE WHO HAVE BEGUN TO MASTER THEIR EXTRAORDINARY POWERS.

THE ASSEMBLY WAS INTERRUPTED BY A THUNDEROUS BOOMING SOUND FROM THE BACK OF THE STAGE...

AND GUESS WHO STEPPED IN THE ROOM?!

IT WAS *HEADMASTER CHAOS* FROM THE INSTITUTE. HE BLASTED A HOLE IN THE WALL WITH HIS ENORMOUS STONE FISTS. WITH HIM WAS HIS NEW STAR PUPIL—PAUSE.

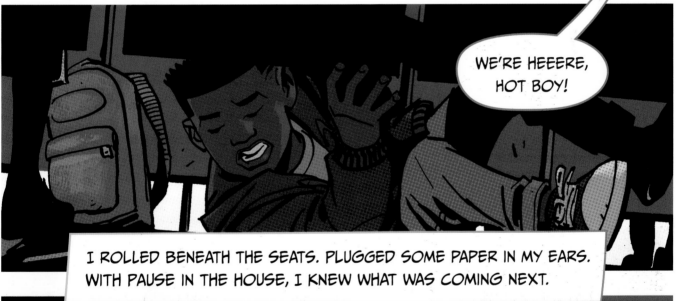

I ROLLED BENEATH THE SEATS. PLUGGED SOME PAPER IN MY EARS. WITH PAUSE IN THE HOUSE, I KNEW WHAT WAS COMING NEXT.

PAUSE SNATCHED THE MIC FROM PRINCIPAL WESTVIEW AND ADDRESSED THE STUDENT BODY... AND SURPRISINGLY, SOME KIDS CHEERED.

THEN SHE LET OUT THE SWEETEST, SHRILLEST CASCADE OF NOTES YOU'D EVER WANT TO HEAR... OR NOT.

THE AUDIENCE FROZE! THEIR BODIES WERE MOTIONLESS, BUT THEIR EYES RACED BACK AND FORTH IN THEIR HEADS LIKE THEY WERE WATCHING A TENNIS MATCH. IT WAS CREEPY.

COME ON OUT, HOT BOY!

YOU BELONG WITH US!

YOU'RE AN OUTCAST, DON'T YOU KNOW THAT?

THAT MADE ME SO MAD, I FELT THAT SURGE OF SCORCHING LAVA RACING THROUGH ME.

BUT YOU KNOW WHAT? THERE'S *NOTHING* WRONG WITH ME. NOTHING AT ALL.

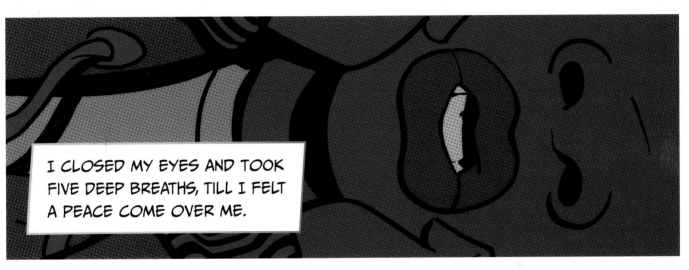

I CLOSED MY EYES AND TOOK FIVE DEEP BREATHS, TILL I FELT A PEACE COME OVER ME.

AND THEN I STOOD UP AND GLARED AT HEADMASTER CHAOS.

GET MY NAME RIGHT— *BOBBY. BEACON.*

WHATEVER...
THERE HE IS! DO WHAT
YOU DO BEST, PAUSE.

PAUSE CUPPED HER HANDS AROUND HER MOUTH AND TRIED
SHOOTING MORE OF THOSE HYPNOTIC NOTES AT ME.

SCH-KRAK

I HELD UP MY FOREARM, AND A SHIELD MADE OF HARDENED LAVA FORMED, WHICH
BOUNCED THE SOUND RIGHT BACK TO HER. (I HAD NO IDEA THAT I COULD DO THAT!)

SHE INSTANTLY FROZE LIKE A STATUE.
PAUSE WAS TEMPORARILY—PAUSED.

THEN I PUT MY PALMS TOGETHER AND AIMED THEM AT HEADMASTER CHAOS.

FWOOOSH

AN ENORMOUS BEAM OF GOLDEN LAVA SHOT AT HIS STONE FISTS AND WELDED THEM TOGETHER.

SHMMM KRK KRK

HE COULDN'T DO ANYTHING BUT DROP TO THE COLD, HARD FLOOR.

DEFEATED.

MISS BROOKLYN RAN UP TO ME AND GAVE ME THE BIGGEST HUG, THE KIND OF HUG THAT MY MOM WOULD GIVE ME.

YOU WERE BRILLIANT, BOBBY, AS USUAL. *PEACE, BE STILL...*

AT THAT MOMENT, I REALIZED THAT AS LONG AS YOU HAVE SOMEONE WHO BELIEVES IN YOU AND APPRECIATES EVERYTHING FROM YOUR TOES TO THE TINY FLAMES ON THE TIPS OF YOUR HAIR, YOU CAN BECOME ANYTHING IN THIS GREAT BIG WORLD.

AND MOST OF ALL, YOU ARE NEEDED, YOU ARE LOVED...

AND EVENTUALLY, YOU'LL END UP RIGHT WHERE YOU'RE SUPPOSED TO BE.

PEACE, BE STILL.